COOKING
with the
GRINCH

by Tish Rabe
illustrated by Tom Brannon

Random House 🏠 New York

The Grinch goes down.

Down to the town.

He hears the bells.

Ding! Dong!

Dong! Ding!

He hears the *Whos*.

They sing!

Sing! Sing!

9

He taps a door.

It's Cindy-Lou!

12

She likes to cook.

The Grinch does too.

He likes to mix.

She likes to stir.

She cooks with him.

He cooks with her.

They make some treats
and start to bake.
Who will eat the
treats they make?

Max! Oh no!

No, no, no, NO!

Max! You have to
go, go, GO!

The treats are done.

Don't let them tip!

23

Oh no! The treats!
They start to slip!

Cindy-Lou is fast!

The treats do not fall.

She saves the treats.

She saves them all.

Merry Christmas, Max!
Yum, yum, yum,
yummy!

The treats are now . . .

. . . in Max's tummy!